Silly Sea Life
FIND IT! COLOR IT!

Diana Zourelias

DOVER PUBLICATIONS, INC.
MINEOLA, NEW YORK

Put on your detective hat and see if you can find the sea life image that doesn't belong among the other things on each page. Be on the lookout for a cleverly hidden angelfish, goldfish, octopus, and even a hammerhead shark! If you can't seem to spot one of the hidden sea creatures, solutions are provided at the end of the book, following plate 29. For added fun, color each of the amusing illustrations with crayons or colored pencils. The cover image with the answer shown is an example of the activities included inside this book.

Bibliographical Note

Silly Sea Life: Find It! Color It! is a new work,
first published by Dover Publications, Inc., in 2016.

International Standard Book Number

ISBN-13: 978-0-486-81095-9
ISBN-10: 0-486-81095-X

Manufactured in the United States
81095X01   2016
www.doverpublications.com

Find the Angelfish

Find the Anglerfish

Find the Blowfish

Find the Clown Fish

Find the Crab

Find the Dolphin

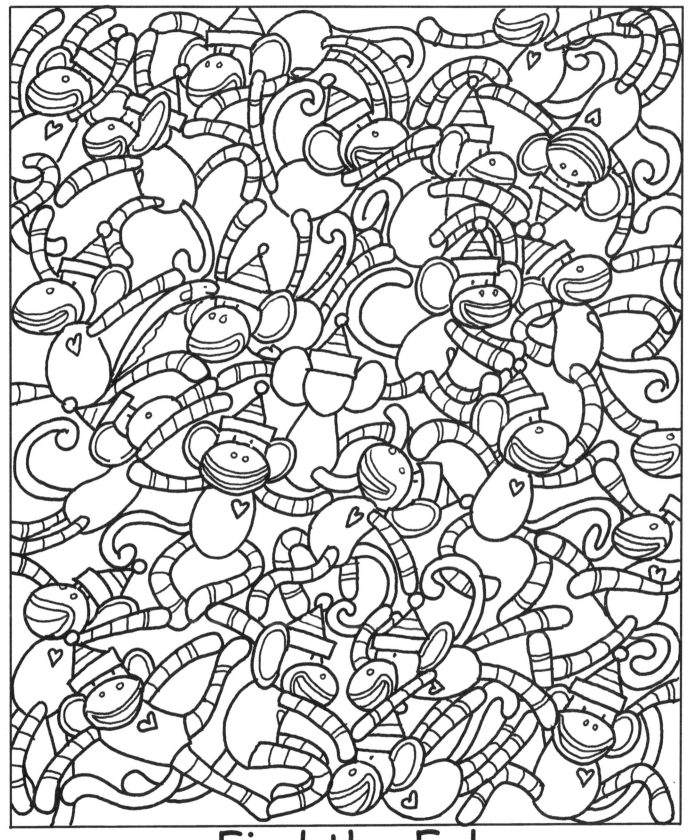

Find the Eel

Find the Goldfish

Find the Hammerhead Shark

Find the Jellyfish

Find the Lionfish

Find the Octopus

Find the Otter

Find the Oyster

Find the Pelican

Find the Sailfish

Find the Sea Horse

Find the Sea Turtle

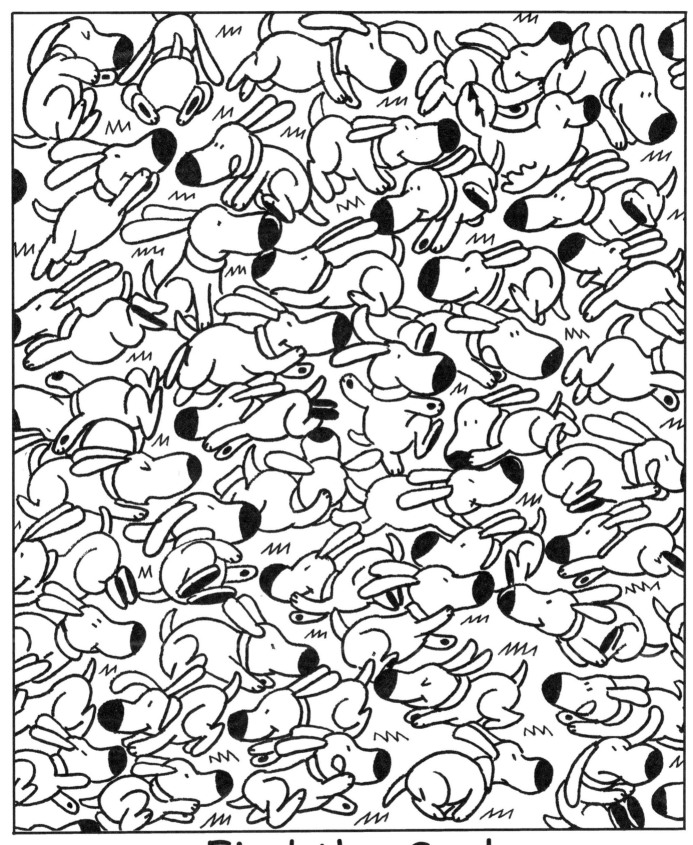

Find the Seal

Find the Seashell

Find the Shark

Find the Shrimp

Find the Squid

Find the Starfish

Find the Stingray

Find the Surgeonfish

Find the Swordfish

Find the Walrus

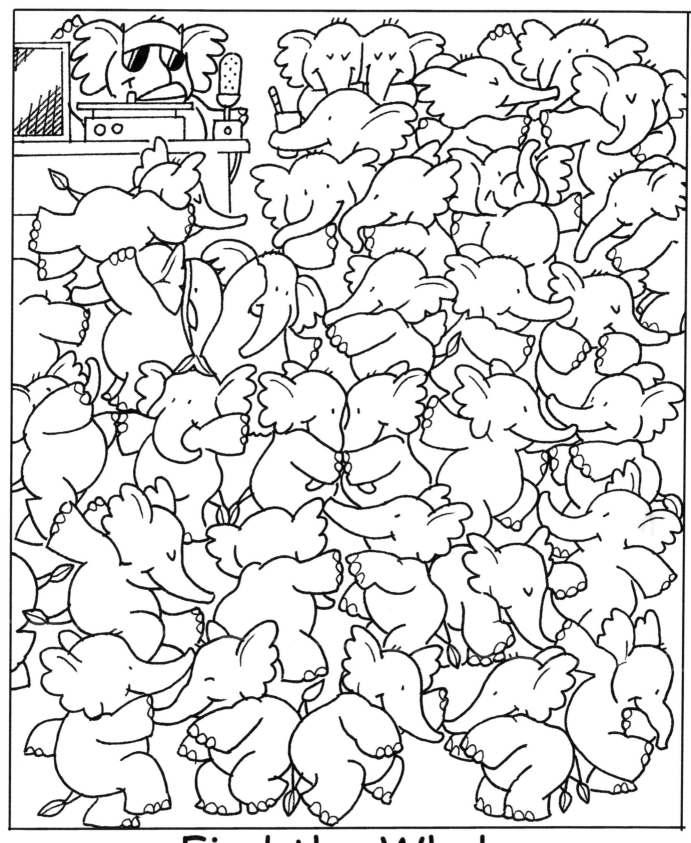

Find the Whale

SOLUTIONS

1 Find the Angelfish

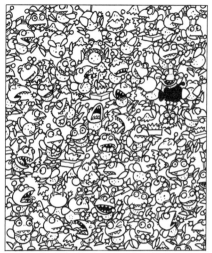

2 Find the Anglerfish

3 Find the Blowfish

4 Find the Clown Fish

5 Find the Crab

6 Find the Dolphin

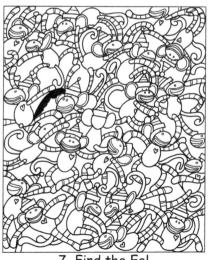

7 Find the Eel

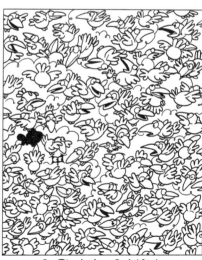

8 Find the Goldfish

9 Find the Hammerhead Shark

10 Find the Jellyfish

11 Find the Lionfish

12 Find the Octopus

13 Find the Otter

14 Find the Oyster

15 Find the Pelican

16 Find the Sailfish

17 Find the Sea Horse

18 Find the Sea Turtle

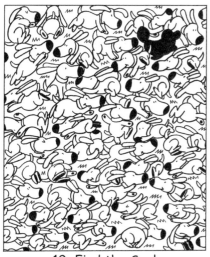

19 Find the Seal

20 Find the Seashell

21 Find the Shark

22 Find the Shrimp

23 Find the Squid

24 Find the Starfish

25 Find the Stingray

26 Find the Surgeonfish

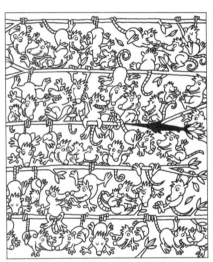

27 Find the Swordfish

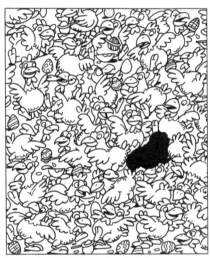

28 Find the Walrus

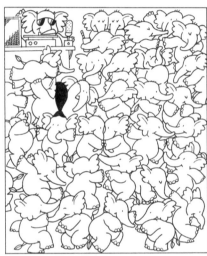

29 Find the Whale